Sam Kinny's an Eating Machine!

Ever since strange Aunt Sylvie put some weird spice in his dinner, Sam has been on a *see*-food diet. Anything he sees, he eats!

And he can't stop—even when he finds himself eating the grossest things ever! Like dog food, dirt—and bugs!

Sam must find out what's happening to him—and how to stop it. If not, he may keep eating and eating and getting bigger and bigger—until he *explodes!*

Also from R. L. Stine

The Beast
The Beast 2

R. L. Stine's Ghosts of Fear Street

Available from MINSTREL Books

THE BOY WHO
ATE FEAR STREET

A Parachute Press Book

A
MINSTREL®
BOOK

Published by POCKET BOOKS
New York   London   Toronto   Sydney   Tokyo   Singapore

A MINSTREL PAPERBACK *Original*

A Minstrel Paperback published by
POCKET BOOKS, a division of Simon & Schuster Inc.
1230 Avenue of the Americas, New York, NY 10020

Copyright © 1996 by Parachute Press, Inc.

THE BOY WHO ATE FEAR STREET WRITTEN BY STEPHEN ROOS

ISBN: 0-671-00183-3

First Minstrel Books paperback printing August 1996

10 9 8 7 6 5 4 3 2 1

FEAR STREET is a registered trademark of
Parachute Press, Inc.

A MINSTREL BOOK and colophon are registered trademarks
of Simon & Schuster Inc.

Cover art by Broeck Steadman

Printed in the U.S.A.

R·L·STINE'S
GHOSTS OF FEAR STREET ®

THE BOY WHO ATE FEAR STREET

"Sam, you have to come over right now," my best friend Kevin pleaded with me over the phone.

"For the tenth time, Kevin—I'm not coming over if you don't tell me *why.*"

"I already told you," Kevin replied. "I can't tell you. Then it wouldn't be a surprise."

My name is Sam Kinny, and the first thing you should know about me is—I hate surprises. Why? I don't know why. I just do.

Another thing I hate is when people pinch my cheeks.

Mom and Dad's friends are always pinching my cheeks. Some of my teachers do it too. Maybe it's because I have a totally round face, straight blond hair, big blue eyes, and long eyelashes. And worst of all, my cheeks are really rosy. Everyone says I'm soooo cute. Then they pinch my cheeks.

Nobody ever pinches Kevin's cheeks. Kevin looks tough—just the way I want to look.

Kevin has brown hair and it always looks messy. And he has a little scar on his right cheek, where his sister Lissa scratched him accidentally while they were practicing karate.

"Sam, you have to come over," Kevin begged. "My mom started dinner—and she's cooking all your favorites."

"Really?" I asked. "Macaroni and cheese? And rice pudding for dessert with white raisins and marshmallows?"

"Yep," Kevin replied. "All white food. As usual."

"What do you mean, as usual?" I protested. "I don't *always* eat white food."

"Oh, yeah?" Kevin challenged me. "Name one food you eat that isn't white. Come on, name one."

"Coke," I said. "I love Coke, and Coke isn't white. It's brown."

"You never drink Coke," Kevin reminded me. "You drink Sprite. That's white, practically."

Okay. What can I say? Kevin was right. I eat only white food. Why?

I know the answer to this one.

Because that's what I like.

Some of my friends think eating only white food is weird. But Lissa doesn't think so. That's because she eats the exact same thing for lunch every single day. Peanut butter and jelly. She never eats anything else for lunch—ever.

"So—you're coming over. Right?" Kevin asked.

"I guess so," I gave in. Macaroni and cheese is my favorite food. *No way* could I pass it up. Even if it meant going to Kevin's house for a surprise.

I ran downstairs and grabbed my jacket from the hall closet. Then I went into the kitchen to tell Mom where I was going.

Mom sat at the kitchen table sewing blond hair on a big doll. Fred, my collie, sat at her feet. Fred loves watching Mom make her dolls.

Mom makes lots of dolls. And she's really good at it. She makes them in all sizes—little ones, big ones, some as tall as I am. She sells them all over the country. People really love her dolls.

"Mom, I'm going over to the Sullivans' house for dinner. They're having macaroni and cheese. Okay?" Mom knows how much I love macaroni and cheese.

"Sure." Mom glanced up and smiled.

"Dinner?" Dad walked into the room carrying a screwdriver. "Is it time for dinner already?"

"Almost," Mom said. "I'll start dinner just as soon as you tighten my left elbow."

"No problem!" Dad replied.

He leaned over and tightened the doll's elbow—not Mom's. Dad is really handy. He can fix anything.

"See you!" I called as I walked out the back door.

I thought about the macaroni and cheese—and ran the four blocks to Kevin's house. When I arrived, Kevin and Lissa were practicing karate on the front lawn.

"Kow! Dar! Fing!" Lissa shouted.

"Kwon! Fo! Tow!" Kevin shouted back.

They moved around each other, making circles in the air with their hands. Then in one swift motion Lissa lunged for Kevin and flipped him onto his back.

Lissa is eleven, a year younger than Kevin and me. But she's a lot stronger than either of us. She has long brown hair, big brown eyes, and freckles that dot her nose. She hates her freckles as much as I hate my rosy cheeks.

"Hey! Where did you learn that move?" Kevin muttered, sitting up and rubbing his back.

"From Aunt Sylvie." Lissa grinned.

"Who's Aunt Sylvie?" I asked.

"Thanks a lot, Lissa." Kevin grumbled. "Now you ruined the surprise."

4

"It's not my fault." Lissa blew her long bangs out of her eyes. "You're the one who asked about my new move."

"Hey, guys. Who is Aunt Sylvie?" I asked again.

"She's our great-aunt," Kevin explained. "She's staying with us for a few months. She was the surprise."

"Your great-aunt is the surprise?" I asked in disbelief. "What kind of surprise is that?"

"Oh, Aunt Sylvie is totally incredible," Lissa boasted.

"You've never met anyone like her!" Kevin added. "The last time we saw her, we were babies. So we didn't know how great Great-Aunt Sylvie was—till now!"

"Come on." Kevin jumped to his feet. "You have to meet her!" He led the way into the house.

"What's that smell?" I asked, sniffing the air as we walked toward the kitchen.

"Aunt Sylvie must be cooking up something special," Kevin answered.

Special might be one way to describe the smell of Aunt Sylvie's cooking. *Putrid* would be another.

"There she is," Lissa whispered as we stood in the doorway to the kitchen.

When I saw Aunt Sylvie standing at the stove, I could tell right away that she was different from any other aunt I had met before.

5

I mean, she looked like a grandmother—kind of old with white hair and wrinkled skin. But she was wearing bright pink leggings, a neon-orange sweatshirt, and black hightops. And she wore a blue baseball cap with the visor turned to the back, just the way I wear mine.

She stood in front of a huge pot, stirring whatever was inside it with a long wooden spoon.

Rows and rows of herbs, spices, and knobby hard things that looked like plant roots sat on the counter next to the stove. She reached for one of the roots and started to drop it into the pot. Then she stopped.

"No orrisroot?" she asked. "Oh! Of course not! You're absolutely right! Orrisroot is for making perfume—not dinner!" Aunt Sylvie hit her forehead with the heel of her hand. "How forgetful I am!"

I craned my neck and glanced around the room. Except for Aunt Sylvie, no one was there.

"Who is she talking to?" I whispered.

"Oh, Aunt Sylvie likes to talk to the dead," Kevin answered. "She says they're full of good advice."

"She *what?*" I shouted.

Aunt Sylvie whirled around. "Hi, kids! Dinner is almost ready!"

6

"Aunt Sylvie, this is our friend Sam," Lissa introduced me. "He's going to eat dinner with us tonight."

I backed away from the kitchen doorway. *No way* was I going to eat what was in that pot. *NO WAY!*

Kevin grabbed my arm and pulled me forward. "Come on. You have to talk to Aunt Sylvie. She is awesome."

"Wouldn't she rather talk to my great-grandfather?" I whispered, trying to tug free. "He's dead. I'll introduce her to him. But I have to go home first—to find out his name."

"Sam, don't be shy." Aunt Sylvie walked over to me. Then she slowly reached up to my face with her wrinkled fingers—and pinched my cheeks. "You are soooo cute!"

Kevin and Lissa giggled.

Aunt Sylvie chuckled too as she guided me to the stove. She picked up the wooden spoon and started stirring the pot again.

"How about a little taste?" she asked, smiling.

"NO! I mean, no, thank you," I said, backing away—before I gagged from the smell.

Aunt Sylvie caught my hand. "Come. Come. Just a little taste!" she urged.

She lifted the spoon out of the pot.

And I gasped.

A slimy creature with arms and legs stared up at me. I watched in horror as it tried to wriggle off the spoon.

"Just a taste," Aunt Sylvie repeated.

She shoved the spoon against my lips.

I clenched my lips shut. I shook my head no, furiously.

Aunt Sylvie tightened her grasp on my wrist.

She stared hard into my eyes.

"I insist!" she said. "Open wide—NOW!"

2

"**N**ooooo!" I shouted as loud as I could.

I yanked my hand from Aunt Sylvie's grasp and ran for the hall.

But Kevin and Lissa blocked the kitchen doorway.

"Hey, Sam!" Kevin grabbed my shoulders. "Get a grip. You don't have to taste it if you don't want to."

I glanced over my shoulder. Aunt Sylvie stood by the stove, smiling at me.

"That's right, Sam," Aunt Sylvie said. "I just thought you might enjoy it. It's a special recipe I learned on a small island in the South Pacific. Squid stew. Very tasty."

"Sam doesn't really like to try new things," Lissa explained. "He eats only plain old white food."

Aunt Sylvie narrowed her eyes at me. "You must eat more than that," she said.

"No. No, I don't," I admitted.

"You don't understand, Sam." Her smile turned cold. "That wasn't a question—you *must* eat more than that."

Aunt Sylvie turned her back and stirred the pot.

"Come on," Kevin pulled me out in the hallway. "I want you to see something upstairs."

Kevin and Lissa thought Aunt Sylvie was awesome. I thought she was creepy.

"What do you want me to see?" I asked as we climbed the stairs.

"Aunt Sylvie's room," Kevin replied. "It's full of the most incredible stuff you've ever seen."

We stepped into Aunt Sylvie's room. Just a few days earlier it had been a regular bedroom—with pictures on the walls, a big bed with an oak headboard, and a colorful rug on the floor.

Now everything was gone. Even the bed.

"Where does she sleep?" I asked.

Kevin pointed to a straw mat on the floor. "Aunt Sylvie doesn't like clutter. She says if you surround yourself with too many things, the spirits will have a hard time finding you."

I made up my mind right then and there to fill my bedroom with as much junk as possible.

"Get this, Sam," Kevin called to me from across the room. He pointed to a wooden mask that hung on the wall. Its mouth twisted into an ugly sneer.

"Pretty spooky," I said, glancing away from the dark eye sockets. They seemed to stare right through me.

"It's not spooky," Lissa said. "It's a medicine mask from an ancient mountain tribe. Aunt Sylvie says when you put it on, it will chase the germs right out of your body if you're sick."

"Does Aunt Sylvie think it really works?" I asked, turning my back to the mask.

"She's not really sure," Kevin replied. "But she says it's important to keep an open mind."

"Yeah," Lissa added. "She says even the impossible is possible—whatever that means."

I wandered around the room, studying Aunt Sylvie's stuff. Tacked on the wall over the sleeping mat I saw an Indian dream catcher. I made one in camp last summer. It's a big wooden hoop with a web made of string inside it. It's supposed to catch bad dreams and let good dreams pass through.

"Sam, check this out!" Lissa held a silver mirror

in front of my face. Just as I caught my reflection in it, Lissa flipped it over.

I gasped.

A dozen black eyes stared back at me!

"The eyes are carved into the wood," Lissa explained. "They look almost real, don't they?"

They looked *totally* real to me, but I nodded in agreement.

I walked around the room some more, studying Aunt Sylvie's collection. On the dresser sat a jar of cold cream and dozens and dozens of crystals. Pink, purple, green, red—all shimmering in the glow of the bedroom lamp's light.

I made my way over to the back of the room—where I spotted an old aquarium.

I peered inside.

It was empty.

"Kids, dinner is ready!" Mrs. Sullivan called from downstairs.

"Let's go!" Lissa declared. "I'm starving."

Lissa and Kevin bolted from the room, shutting the lamp off on the way out.

"Hey, thanks, guys," I said, standing in total darkness.

I walked toward the door—and stepped right on the straw mat.

Oh, no. I'm standing on Aunt Sylvie's bed. With my shoes on. She's not going to like that.

"Sam! Hurry up!" Kevin called from downstairs. "We're really hungry."

"Sure, Kevin," I grumbled. "No problem."

I tiptoed across the mat.

And then I felt it.

Something moving up my leg.

Higher and higher.

I ran the rest of the way across the mat.

I charged into the lighted hall.

I peered down at my leg—and screamed in horror.

"Snaaaaake!"

3

"**A** snake! It's a snake!" I cried out. "Help me!"

All the Sullivans charged up the steps.

"Get it off me!" I shrieked.

I shook my leg as hard as I could. But the snake just coiled around it. Tighter and tighter.

"My leg—it's turning numb!" I shouted. "Get it off!"

"Oh, dear," Aunt Sylvie murmured. She wasn't wearing the baseball cap anymore. Instead, she had two long, pink feathers sticking up from the back of her hair. She shook her head and the feathers fluttered.

"Shirley, how did you get out?" Aunt Sylvie

wagged her finger at the snake. Then she leaned over and uncoiled it from my leg. "It's back to the terrarium for you," she said, kissing the snake on its head.

"Isn't Shirley a cool pet?" Kevin exclaimed.

"Uh, yeah, cool," I said, hoping my voice didn't shake too much.

"I think Shirley frightened Sam." Mrs. Sullivan placed her arm around my shoulders. "We'll make sure Shirley doesn't escape again. Now—let's all go down for dinner."

I wondered if Shirley was poisonous, but I decided it would be better not to ask.

Everyone took their seats at the table. "Come sit by me, Sam." Aunt Sylvie patted the chair next to her. "I'm sorry if Shirley frightened you."

"She didn't," I lied. "She just surprised me, that's all."

"Did you like my little collection?" she asked. "I'm especially fond of the crystals. Some people believe they have healing powers, you know. But I like them mostly for their beautiful colors."

"Aunt Sylvie knows all about things with strange healing powers," Lissa explained.

"And she knows all about the spirit world," Kevin added. "She travels around to lots of countries and collects stories about ancient spirits and magic spells."

15

I could see why Kevin and Lissa thought Aunt Sylvie was cool. I guess it was pretty neat to have a great-aunt who knew all this weird stuff. But I still thought there was something creepy about her.

"And tomorrow I begin my newest study—in Shadyside. It's so exciting—I can't wait." Aunt Sylvie clapped her hands.

"What are you studying in Shadyside?" I asked.

"Fear Street." Aunt Sylvie's eyes lit up. "I've heard so many stories about it. Ghosts in the Fear Street Woods. Haunted tree houses. A mysterious cave where shadow people live.

"I've never actually seen a ghost," Aunt Sylvie continued, "but I've heard that many people in Shadyside have. Oh, it would be so exciting to meet one!"

"I hope you won't be too disappointed," Mr. Sullivan said, chuckling. "We *live* here—and we've never seen a ghost. And Sam actually lives on Fear Street."

"Really, Sam?" Aunt Sylvie shifted her gaze to me. "You live on Fear Street?"

I nodded.

"Well?" Aunt Sylvie stared hard into my eyes.

"Well, what?" I asked, shifting uncomfortably in my chair.

"Have you ever seen a ghost?" she demanded.

"Um, no," I replied. "Everyone says weird things

16

happen to you if you live on Fear Street. But I've lived there my whole life, and nothing weird has ever happened to me."

"That's right, Sam," Mrs. Sullivan said. "I'm afraid they're just stories. Silly stories."

"I'm starving!" Lissa shouted. "Let's eat!"

Mrs. Sullivan removed the cover from a large, steaming bowl of squid stew.

"I—I'm not really hungry," I said, pushing my chair away from the table. "Can I be excused?"

"Of course you're hungry!" Aunt Sylvie exclaimed. "Don't worry, dear. This is not for you. Here is your dinner."

Aunt Sylvie began to remove the lid from a dish in front of her.

I held my breath.

I didn't want to look.

"Macaroni and cheese," Kevin announced when the lid was lifted. "See—I told you my mom was making it for you!"

"We warned Aunt Sylvie that you wouldn't eat her stew," Lissa said. "We explained to her that you're a picky eater."

As I ate my macaroni and cheese, I could feel Aunt Sylvie's eyes on me.

"Sometimes it's smart to be a picky eater," she said thoughtfully.

"What do you mean, Aunt Sylvie?" Lissa asked.

17

"I read a Middle Eastern folktale once about a boy who ate the same thing for breakfast, lunch, and dinner—white rice and beets. That's all he would eat.

"One day he and two boys from his village took a walk in the woods—where they discovered a most unusual berry bush. It had bright red leaves. And on each leaf hung a tiny black berry. Smaller than a pea.

"His friends quickly gobbled a handful of the small berries. They had never tasted anything so sweet, so delicious. They ate and ate until the berry bush was bare.

"Then they headed home—and ate everything in their kitchen cupboards. They wandered through the village, day after day, searching for food. They grew fatter and fatter, but they couldn't stop eating.

"The picky eater couldn't believe what was happening to his friends. He watched in terror as they devoured every last crumb in the village.

"The boys grew so fat that their skin just couldn't take the strain. It couldn't stretch another inch. But that didn't stop them from eating. They traveled to the next village and devoured all the food there. And that's when it happened."

"What happened?" Lissa's eyebrows shot up.

"Those poor boys exploded." Aunt Sylvie nodded

knowingly. "Spilled their insides all over everything."

A piece of macaroni stuck in my throat and I started to choke. Mrs. Sullivan patted me on the back. "What a terrible story!" she exclaimed.

"Yes, I thought so too," Aunt Sylvie agreed. "Now, who wants dessert? I bet you can't wait for dessert, Sam. Right?"

"NO! I mean no, thank you," I replied. "I'm full."

"Nonsense!" Aunt Sylvie said. "I made it especially for you. Rice pudding. Your favorite!"

Aunt Sylvie spooned some rice pudding into a bowl and set it in front of me. Then she stared at me, waiting for me to try it.

I scooped up a tiny bit and ate it. It was delicious. The best rice pudding I ever tasted.

"This is great!" I said, swallowing a big mouthful.

I took another spoonful—this one with a few raisins.

I chewed the raisins—and cried out in horror.

I felt my face turn bright red.

My tongue began to burn.

My mouth was on fire!

4

"**H**elp!" I cried, leaping up from my chair. "My mouth is on fire!"

Mrs. Sullivan handed me a glass of milk. I gulped it down. Then I reached over and grabbed Lissa's glass of milk. I gulped that down too.

The burning feeling spread across my lips and down my throat. Even my chest felt scorched, and my tongue began to swell.

I grabbed every glass of milk on the table and gulped it down. Then I snatched the milk container from the kitchen counter and chugged that.

"Are you okay, dear?" Aunt Sylvie asked, patting me on the back.

"What . . . did . . . you . . . put . . . in . . . my . . . pudding?" I sputtered, jerking away from her.

"Aunt Sylvie didn't put anything in your rice pudding," Lissa said. "You probably just swallowed wrong."

The Sullivans and Kevin nodded in agreement, but Aunt Sylvie tapped the side of her forehead with her index finger. "Hmmmm, let me think. Let me think," she repeated over and over again.

While Aunt Sylvie tried to remember, I poked around the top layer of rice pudding with my spoon.

I found rice. I found pudding.

Nothing else.

I poked around some more.

Ah-ha! At the bottom of the bowl I found what I was looking for. Little dark flakes. So little that I thought they were specks of cinnamon at first.

"What's *this?*" I asked Aunt Sylvie, pointing a shaky finger into my bowl.

"Great-Uncle Henry!" Aunt Sylvie exclaimed.

"Huh?"

"Now I remember! While I was making the rice pudding, Great-Uncle Henry visited for a chat," Aunt Sylvie began to explain. "And he suggested that I use the new spice I brought back from the Orient."

Aunt Sylvie held up a bottle of the black flakes.

21

"I enjoyed speaking to Uncle Henry." She sighed. "We've spoken so little since he died."

"Aunt Sylvie," Mrs. Sullivan chided, "you're going to scare the children."

"Oh, nonsense!" Aunt Sylvie chuckled. "The children know what an odd creature I am!"

Everyone at the table laughed. Everyone but me.

"I'm sorry the spice burned your tongue." Aunt Sylvie turned to me. "It's supposed to be tangy— not hot."

"Maybe it turned rotten," I murmured.

Aunt Sylvie reached over for my bowl of rice pudding. She lifted it to her nose and sniffed. "It smells okay, but I bet you're right. It probably has spoiled. I'm going to throw it out—right now."

"Aren't you going to taste it first?" I asked. "Maybe it's not spoiled. Maybe it was just too spicy for me."

"Taste it?" Aunt Sylvie gasped. "Oh, no! *I'm* not going to taste it."

5

"**W**hat?" I shouted. Why aren't you going to taste it?" I leaped up from my chair.

Aunt Sylvie didn't reply.

She headed toward the sink and emptied the jar of flakes down the drain.

"Why didn't you taste it?" I demanded.

"Oh, those flakes are much too strong for me!" Aunt Sylvie smiled. "I don't care for tangy food myself. Now, who would like some vanilla ice cream? I bet you would, Sam. Right?"

* * *

Everyone ate the ice cream except me. Those black specks in the ice cream were probably vanilla beans—but I wasn't taking any chances.

After dinner Kevin, Lissa, and I played Kevin's LaserBlast video game. I usually win—but not this time. My stomach was upset, and I felt weird. Kind of hot all over.

"See you guys tomorrow," I told Kevin and Lissa when it was time to leave.

"Great!" Kevin walked me to the front door. "Aunt Sylvie has some more awesome things you've got to see!"

"And maybe she'll let us play with Shirley!" Lissa called from the den.

I didn't think I wanted to see any more of Aunt Sylvie's things—or play with Shirley. I knew for sure that I didn't want to eat any more of her cooking.

When I reached home, my stomach was still upset so I went right up to bed. I snuggled under my blanket, tucked it under my chin, and fell asleep instantly.

I don't know how much later it was when I woke up. But all the lights were out, and Mom and Dad were in bed.

I made my way down the dark hall, down the steps, and into the kitchen. My stomach felt much better—back to normal. Now I was hungry. I knew just what I wanted—my favorite sandwich, mayonnaise on white bread.

A full moon hung in the sky. It lit the kitchen with a warm glow. *I'd better not put the light on,* I thought as I searched the kitchen counter for the bread. *I don't want to wake Mom or Dad.*

After I found the bread I hunted for a new jar of mayonnaise in the pantry—I finished the old jar at lunch. I eat a lot of mayonnaise, about a jar a week. I can't help it. I really love the stuff!

I stifled a yawn, then, half asleep, I made my sandwich. When it was ready, I sunk my teeth in for a really big bite.

Delicious.

Plain old white food—without a single one of Aunt Sylvie's spices from around the world.

I took another bite. And another. And another.

I needed something to drink.

I opened the refrigerator and grabbed a bottle of Sprite.

The light from the refrigerator fell on the kitchen counter.

On my half-eaten sandwich.

I stared at the sandwich.

Something was wrong with it. Very wrong.

25

I rubbed my eyes and focused. I stared at it again, harder this time. Something still didn't seem right.

I lowered my face to the counter.

I squinted closely at the sandwich.

And screamed.

6

Sponges! Not bread!

I made a sandwich with two moldy green sponges. And I ate it. And it tasted good.

How could I have made a sponge sandwich? How could I have eaten it? HOW?

The room began to spin. I grabbed hold of the kitchen counter to steady myself.

That's when I saw the yellow ooze seeping out from my sponge sandwich.

Oh, no, I moaned. *What did I spread inside those slices?*

I didn't want to look, but I had to.

I lifted the top sponge. My hand shook.

The yellow ooze ran off the sponge and dripped along the counter, and my stomach lurched

I dipped my finger into it. Sniffed it.

It smelled lemony. Soapy.

Lemon-Fresh Dish Detergent.

I just ate a soap and sponge sandwich. And I liked it.

What is wrong with me? How could I have eaten that?

I quickly tossed the sponges into the trash and ran upstairs to my bedroom. I dove under the covers and stared out my bedroom window at the dark, cloudless sky.

I asked myself over and over again, *How could I have eaten that? How? How? How?*

And then the answer came to me.

I was sleepwalking. That had to be it. I dreamed that I was hungry, and I sleepwalked into the kitchen and made myself a sandwich.

The light from the refrigerator woke me up—and that's when I realized what I was doing.

It really did make sense. Mom says Dad walks in his sleep all the time.

I felt better.

I leaned back against my pillow, closed my eyes, and fell asleep.

* * *

28

"Sam! Time to get up!" Mom called up the stairs. "Time for breakfast!"

I pulled on my favorite navy blue T-shirt and my favorite jeans, the ones with the rip in the knee. I slipped on my sneakers and ran downstairs without tying the laces. Mom always yells at me for that. She says one day I'm going to trip and break my neck. Mothers say that kind of stuff to their kids.

I sat down at the kitchen table and took a big swallow of milk. "YUCK!"

"What's wrong, Sam?" Dad asked.

"The milk is sour!" I grumbled. "It tastes disgusting."

"It must be past the expiration date," Mom said. "And I just bought it yesterday. I'm going to bring it back to the grocery store and lodge a complaint." She rummaged through the garbage for the empty container.

She took the container from the trash. Then she lifted out the two green sponges. The two half-eaten green sponges.

I held my breath as she studied them.

No way was I going to admit I ate a sponge sandwich last night—even if I did do it in my sleep.

"Hey, Mom!" I tried to steal Mom's attention. "Aren't you going to check the expiration date on the milk?"

My plan didn't work.

29

Mom continued to stare at the sponges.

"Mom! I'm starving! What's for breakfast? I'm going to be late for school."

That worked.

She tossed the sponges back into the garbage. "How about some Cream of Wheat?" she asked. A smile formed on her lips. Mom knows that's my all-time-favorite breakfast.

I nodded eagerly. Sometimes I eat two bowls of Cream of Wheat a day, one in the morning and one when I come home from school.

Mom set one bowl in front of me and one in front of Dad. Dad likes Cream of Wheat almost as much as I do.

White puffs of steam floated up from my cereal bowl. Ahhhh, I thought, Cream of Wheat—so nice, so white.

I couldn't wait to eat it. I really was starving.

I dipped my spoon into the bowl.

I slipped the spoon into my mouth.

The Cream of Wheat slid off onto my tongue—and my jaw dropped open in horror.

"Dad!" I screamed. "Don't eat the Cream of Wheat! *DON'T!*"

7

Too late.

Dad swallowed a huge spoonful of Cream of Wheat.

"Dad, the Cream of Wheat . . ."

". . . is delicious!" Dad finished. "What's the problem, Sam? Is there something wrong with yours?"

"It—it tastes gross," I stammered. "Like sand mixed with vinegar." I turned to my mom. "What did you do to *my* Cream of Wheat?"

"I didn't do anything to it," Mom answered. "I made it the way I always do. Half a cup of Cream of Wheat and a half cup of boiling water."

"You must have done something different to it, Mom," I insisted.

"No, Sam, I didn't."

"Well, someone did," I argued. "It tastes awful."

Fred trotted into the room. He set his head down in my lap. He does that every morning, waiting for me to share some of my breakfast with him.

I placed some Cream of Wheat on my finger.

I watched closely as Fred licked it off.

Mom and Dad watched too.

Fred licked every last drop off, then wagged his tail, begging for more.

I let out a low sigh.

"Try something else," Dad suggested. "How about some mayonnaise on white bread?"

"NO! I mean, no, thank you. I'm not hungry anymore."

I shoved my chair back and headed into the living room. I checked the clock over the fireplace. There was still time before I had to leave for school. I could catch a cartoon. I headed for the TV.

I turned it on and—zzpt!

A small shock ran through my hand. Static electricity.

I shook my hand, trying to stop the tingling. I sat down on the couch. Fred jumped into my lap and scratched at his flea bites. Fred loves to explore the

Fear Street Woods—but the only thing he seems to find there are fleas.

I stroked Fred's head and—zzpt. Zapped again.

I gave Fred a hard shove and he jumped off my lap. He gazed up at me sadly. "Sorry, boy," I apologized. "I know it wasn't your fault."

I gave Fred a big hug, then grabbed my backpack and left for school.

I spotted Kevin and Lissa walking up the school steps. "Hey, guys. Wait up," I called.

As we reached the door, the first bell rang. I grabbed the doorknob—and zzzpt! My whole body shook. A powerful jolt ran from my head right down to my toes.

"Oooow!" I cried out, shaking my arms and legs. "I don't believe this!"

"What's the big deal?" Lissa asked. "It's just static electricity."

"Yeah, but this is the third time I got shocked this morning," I explained. "And this one really hurt." I could still feel the tingling in my toes and fingertips. "Don't you think that's weird—getting shocked three times in one morning?"

"Shocking!" Lissa joked.

"Ha-ha, Lissa. Real funny." I turned to Kevin, but he just shrugged his shoulders. I guess he didn't think it was such a big deal either.

And maybe it wasn't.

Maybe I was just in a weird mood. I mean, wouldn't you be if you ate a sponge sandwich?

"I have to stop at my locker first," I told Kevin. Kevin and I are in the same class. "See you inside."

I grabbed my notebook from my locker and ran to my classroom. I found Kevin waiting for me outside the door.

"Why didn't you go in?" I asked.

"I have an idea," he whispered. "Touch Lucas on the back of his neck. See if you get a shock."

"Why?" I asked, confused. "You said the shock thing was no big deal."

"I didn't say that," he reminded me. "Lissa did. Maybe something weird *is* going on with you," he went on. "Lucas wears braces. Let's see if you get a shock from them."

I sat down at my desk. Lucas Johnson sits directly in front of me. Since school started three months ago, I'd seen a lot of the back of his neck, but I never felt like touching it. And I didn't feel like touching it now.

I glanced sideways at Kevin. He nodded his head, urging me on.

I'll just brush the back of Lucas's neck, I thought. Then when Lucas turns around, I'll apologize. Pretend it was an accident.

I leaned forward.

34

I reached out my fingers.

Even though I was pretty sure nothing would happen, my hand started shaking.

I moved it closer.

I glanced at Kevin. "Hurry up!" he mouthed. "Do it now!"

I moved my hand closer—it was an inch away from the back of Lucas's head.

Then I did it. I touched Lucas's neck.

Lucas jerked in his chair.

His entire body stiffened.

Then he began to quake—as if he had been struck by lightning.

He lurched to one side and fell over.

The whole class gasped as he crashed to the floor.

8

"Lucas! Lucas!" I jumped out of my seat. I knelt over Lucas's trembling body. "Help!" I cried out. "Somebody, help him." I gripped Lucas's shoulders, trying to stop his body from jerking.

It didn't work. The harder I held Lucas, the more his body twitched.

"You jerk!" Kevin cried.

"Don't call him a jerk!" I shouted. "Can't you see he's hurt?"

"You," he said, pointing—at me. Then he burst out laughing.

Lucas started laughing too.

My hands dropped from Lucas's shoulders.

"Very funny," I said, taking my seat. "You guys are a riot." I glanced around the classroom. All the kids around us giggled.

"Aw, come on," Lucas said. "Kevin told me about the shocks. Lighten up. It was just a joke. Admit it—it was funny."

I couldn't believe it. I really thought I electrocuted Lucas. I guess it was pretty funny. I even managed to laugh a little later when I thought about it again. And I started to feel a better.

And then it was time for lunch.

And everything turned worse.

Much worse.

As soon as the bell rang for lunch, all the kids shoved their books into their desks and ran for the cafeteria. Even though I didn't eat breakfast, I just wasn't all that hungry. I took my time putting my things away.

"Come on, Sam," Kevin called from the classroom door. "Hurry up. We don't want to get stuck at the end of the food line. There won't be any chips left!"

Kevin loves potato chips. He eats three bags every day with his lunch.

"You go ahead," I called back. "I'm not really hungry."

"You're still mad at me," Kevin declared. "Right? Because of the shock thing?"

"No," I assured him. "I'm just not hungry. Go ahead without me."

Kevin shrugged. I watched him walk toward the cafeteria.

"Sam?" Ms. Munson poked her head into the classroom. "Are you all right, Sam?"

Ms. Munson is the new art teacher at Shadyside. She used to teach art at the Shadyside ABC School. That's a school for toddlers.

Our first art assignment this year was to draw the American flag—using finger paints. I guess Ms. Munson's not used to teaching middle school yet.

"Aren't you going to eat lunch today?" Ms. Munson asked.

"I'm not really hungry," I told her.

"You're not sick, are you?" she asked.

"No. I'm just not hungry," I repeated.

"Are you sure?" she asked.

I didn't know if she meant was I sure I wasn't hungry or was I sure I wasn't sick, but I nodded yes anyway.

"Good!" she exclaimed. "I need your help. Follow me!"

I followed Ms. Munson into the hallway, where she had pasted up a huge banner on the wall. SHADYSIDE MIDDLE SCHOOL SALUTES AUTUMN! it read in big block letters.

"I've cut out all these pretty paper leaves." Ms. Munson pointed to a stack of colorful leaves on the floor. "But I don't have time to paste them on the banner. Are you a good paster?"

"Uh, sure," I answered.

"Won-der-ful," Ms. Munson sang out. She handed me a brush and a big mayonnaise jar filled with paste. "Now, if you need me, I'll be in the art room, cutting out Pilgrim hats for Thanksgiving. You're going to look soooo cute in a Pilgrim hat."

As Ms. Munson walked down the hall, I unscrewed the lid. I dipped the brush into the jar and slopped the back of a red leaf with the paste.

I stuck the leaf to the banner. I held it there for a few seconds. Then I stood back. Hey! It looked pretty good.

I slapped some paste on the back of a gold leaf. The smell of the paste filled my nostrils. To tell you the truth, it didn't smell too good. It smelled, you know, pastey.

But I had to taste it.

I lifted the brush to my lips.

Eat paste? What's wrong with you?

I quickly dropped the brush into the jar.

I took a deep breath—and inhaled the smell of the paste again.

I stared down at the jar.

Just one little taste, I thought. That's all I'll take.
I lifted the brush out of the jar.

Whoa. Wait a minute, I ordered myself. *What are you doing?*

I mean, if I were starving, maybe then I'd eat paste. Maybe. But I'd have to be really hungry to do that.

I slapped the gold leaf on the banner. Then I picked up the next leaf from the pile and brushed the paste on it.

I pasted lots more leaves. I studied the banner. A really nice job, I thought. Really nice.

I peered up and down the hall, searching for someone to admire my work.

No one in sight.

Hmmm. No one in sight.

I scooped out a glob of paste—and shoved it into my mouth.

I swallowed it.

It tasted disgusting.

But I did it again.

I scooped out another glob—a bigger glob this time—and down it went.

Scoop and swallow. Scoop and swallow.

I swallowed globs of paste. I crammed handful after handful into my mouth.

I licked my fingers clean.

40

I filled my mouth with more and more paste.

It stuck to my teeth and spilled out between my lips.

I couldn't stop shoving it in.

Until I heard the voice behind me shriek, "Sam! WHAT ARE YOU EATING?"

9

I whirled around.

"Sam." Kevin stared at me in disbelief. "What are you doing?"

My heart pounded in my chest.

I glanced down at my palm. A glob of paste sat in the middle of it.

I lifted my hand—and stuffed the paste in my mouth.

"Sam!" Kevin shrieked. "Stop!"

I broke out in a cold sweat.

I wanted to stop, but I couldn't. I shoved another handful of paste in my mouth.

Kevin's eyes filled with disgust. He yanked the jar from my hand. I tried to grab it back.

"Why are you eating paste?" Kevin demanded.

"I—I thought it was mayonnaise," I blurted out. Kevin rolled his eyes.

"Okay, I knew it was paste." I shifted nervously from one foot to another. "So what? Lots of kids eat paste."

"No one eats paste after kindergarten, Sam!" Kevin declared.

"Well, I was hungry," I lied. "And it was too late to go to the cafeteria."

Kevin stared at me, trying to decide whether to believe me or not. I could tell he didn't, but he handed the jar back to me. "Come on," he said, avoiding my gaze. "We're going to be late for gym."

I returned the jar of paste to the art room. Then we headed to the gym. As we changed into our gym clothes, I caught Kevin stealing glances at me and shaking his head. He didn't mention the paste again, but I knew he was thinking about it.

I sure was. As I tied my sneaker laces my hands began to tremble.

I ate a half a jar of paste? And I couldn't stop. What is wrong with me?

"Move it, boys. Bleachers today! Everyone out of the locker room. NOW!" Mr. Sirk's voice cut through my thoughts. Mr. Sirk is the gym teacher. He works out with weights a lot—and he looks it. He walks around with his chest puffed out to show off. I don't mind though. I'd puff my chest out, too, if I looked like Mr. Sirk.

I jogged into the gym. I love running the bleachers. I'm the best in the class. I could run them all day.

"We ran the bleachers twice last week," Chris Hassler complained.

"We'll do them twice this week too," Mr. Sirk announced sternly.

"Can't we play football instead?" Zack Pepper asked.

"You boys aren't in shape yet," Mr. Sirk replied. "You've got to get rid of that summer flab. Nothing like running the bleachers to do that. Shape you up in half the time of anything else."

I liked the sound of that. This year I really wanted to shape up. I know if I had muscles like Mr. Sirk and a scar like Kevin's, I'd really look tough.

Zack and Chris grumbled, but they didn't argue. There was no point in arguing with Mr. Sirk. He never changed his mind.

"Ready, guys?" Mr. Sirk shouted.

"Ready!" we yelled back.

"Go!"

We all sprinted to the bleachers. One, two, three, four—I flew up the first four rows and took the lead easily.

Five, six, seven, eight—no problem. I was flying! I could hear the other kids behind me, huffing and puffing. I wasn't even breathing hard.

When I reached the top, I spun around and started down. The rest of the kids still struggled on their way up. I glided by them. As usual, I made it down before everyone else.

"Go for it, Kinny!" Mr. Sirk shouted. "Two more laps!"

Two more laps. No problem. Last week I ran six laps without breaking a sweat.

I started back up as everyone else made their way down. But when I reached the third row, I began breathing hard.

I took two more rows and my heart started to pound. I pushed myself higher and higher. Sweat poured into my eyes.

The other kids started their second laps. A few of them passed me on the way up. What was going on? Nobody *ever* passed me.

I struggled up two more rows, clutching my sides, gasping for air.

"Kinny, are you okay?" Mr. Sirk called.

45

"Just getting my second wind," I answered. I wiped the sweat from my eyes. Then I leaped to the top row—and my legs buckled.

I managed to stay on my feet, but my knees wouldn't stop shaking.

What's wrong with me today? This has never happened before.

My heart began to race wildly.

I tried to calm down, but I couldn't. I pictured myself chomping on the sponge sandwich and eating the paste. *Eating the paste—out of control.*

"Kinny! What are you waiting for?" Mr. Sirk yelled.

My legs trembled as I spun around.

Concentrate! I ordered myself. *Stop thinking and run!*

I stared down at the long rows of bleachers.

I tried to clear my mind.

I lifted my leg to take the first jump—and the gym began to spin.

"Nooooo!" I cried out as my foot missed the bleacher.

I was falling. Falling.

No way to stop.

The next thing I knew, Mr. Sirk was leaning over me. "Kinny! Are you okay?"

"Uh-huh." I nodded, struggling to my feet. "Wh-what happened?"

46

"It looked like you slipped up there," Mr. Sirk replied. "Kevin stopped your fall on his way up."

Kevin stared at me oddly—as if I were a stranger.

"You're usually good for half a dozen laps," Mr. Sirk went on. "What's wrong?"

"I don't know," I answered, confused. "I wish I knew. I really wish I knew."

10

⁓⁓⁓

Kevin and I walked home together after school. "What's with you today?" he said.

"What do you mean?" I asked, feeling uncomfortable.

"What do you mean, what do I mean?" he replied. "You know what I mean."

"Hey, guys! Wait up!" It was Lissa, running up behind us.

"Sam, you have to stop by our house before you go home," she said, out of breath. "You have to see our new karate move. Right, Kevin?"

"Right," Kevin agreed. "Aunt Sylvie said she made contact with the spirit of Bruce Lee last night. She said he showed her one of his incredible moves. Then she taught it to us. She's great at it. Maybe she'll show it to you."

"Can I, um, see it tomorrow? I promised my mom I'd come straight home from school and help her clean out the basement," I lied. My legs still felt wobbly, I wanted to go straight home, and I really didn't feel like seeing Aunt Sylvie today.

"Okay," Lissa said. "But don't forget. You really have to see this one!"

"Sure," I said as I turned the corner to my house. "Tomorrow."

When I walked through my front door, I actually started to feel like my old self again. My legs seemed more solid, and I had my appetite back—my normal appetite, for some real food.

"Mom!" I yelled. "I'm home."

No answer.

"Mom! I'm home!" I yelled louder this time. "I'm hungry."

Still no answer.

"I haven't eaten anything all day, Mom!" I shouted.

No reason to tell her about the paste. Right?

Right.

And I couldn't anyhow. She wasn't home.

I dropped my backpack on the counter and opened the refrigerator. Rye bread, grape jelly, leftover beans. I scanned the shelves and grabbed two hard-boiled eggs.

I sat down at the kitchen table and separated the whites from the yolks. On the chair next to me sat Mom's newest doll—the biggest one she's made so far. It was taller than I am, and it had long red hair and freckles. Almost finished, the only things missing were its eyes.

I bet I know where Mom went, I realized. To find eyes for the doll.

I popped a piece of the egg white into my mouth—and spit it out. It tasted bitter—and gritty. In fact, it scratched my tongue.

There must have been eggshell stuck to it, I realized as I tossed it into the trash. A rotten egg with the shell still stuck to it—yuck.

I bit into the second egg. Ewwww! This one tasted even worse than the first. Kind of slimy and sour.

What was going on?

Why did my milk taste sour? And my Cream of Wheat? And now the eggs?

My stomach let out a loud, complaining rumble.

50

I was starving.

I had to find something to eat that didn't taste terrible.

I checked the refrigerator again—nothing.

I searched the pantry. Canned soup. Crackers. Corn flakes. Chocolate sprinkles. Tuna fish.

I decided to wait for Mom to get home. I'd ask her to make me a big bowl of macaroni and cheese.

My stomach let out another loud rumble.

To take my mind off how hungry I was, I decided to concentrate on my homework. I rummaged through my backpack for my English assignment. I had to read the next three chapters of *Johnny Tremaine*. Ms. Hartman planned a quiz on it tomorrow.

I opened the book. The story takes place in Boston, during the American Revolution. I really like reading that stuff, and I dove right in. When I reached the most exciting part, the part where Johnny burns his hand, I heard the slurping sounds.

I glanced across the kitchen. Fred hung over his bowl, devouring his dog food.

"Hey, Fred! Can you hold it down?"

Fred lifted his head from his bowl and gazed up at me. Drool and dog food dribbled from his mouth onto the floor.

"Fred, that's disgusting," I told him. Fred wagged his tail.

I returned to my book.

Slurp. Slurp.

"Fred, please!"

Fred glanced up again, then plunged his head back into his bowl.

Slurp. Slurp.

The sound of Fred's tongue lapping up his food made me feel queasy.

I leaped up from the chair and pushed his bowl away. "Go into the living room. Go to the window and wait for Mom." I pointed toward the front door.

Fred didn't budge.

"Go!"

Fred inched over to his bowl.

I bent down and moved it farther away—and caught a whiff of his food.

It smelled good—great, actually.

My stomach began to growl. Fred's ears perked up when he heard it—then he edged away from me.

He watched me sink to my hands and knees.

He watched as I lowered my head to his bowl.

He moved in, trying to nudge me away from his food.

I pushed him back, and he began to snarl.

52

He nudged me again.

I pushed him away again.

I lowered my head, closer and closer to the food, breathing in the aroma. The incredibly delicious smell.

And then I dove headfirst into the bowl. My tongue darted out, ready to lap up the juicy beef chunks.

STOP! a voice inside my head screamed. *WHAT ARE YOU DOING?*

I leaped up from the floor and threw myself into the kitchen chair.

I don't believe this! I almost ate Fred's dog food, I thought in horror. I pictured myself hanging over Fred's bowl, and I started to gag. *What is wrong with me? How could I even think about eating dog food?*

Slurp. Slurp.

Fred had returned to his bowl.

The smell of the dog food floated up to my nostrils as he ate.

The delicious smell.

I gripped the table with both hands, forcing myself to stay seated. I held on so tightly, my knuckles turned white.

Fred's slurping grew louder.

I grew hungrier.

I wanted that dog food.

I had to have that dog food.

I wanted it now.

"No! No! NOOO!" I chanted over and over. "I will not eat dog food!"

I held on to the table until Fred finished eating. Then I let go, and my hands began to tremble. I sat on them for a few minutes to make them stop.

I inhaled deeply, then let my breath out slowly.

You are in control, I told myself. *You did not eat the dog food. Now, go back to your book. Everything is okay.*

I forced myself to focus on the words. Fred stretched out in a corner of the kitchen, scratching at his flea bites.

"Here, boy!" I called. "Sorry I pushed you!"

Fred trotted over and plunked down on the floor next to me. I petted him with one hand and turned the page of my book with the other. This was another one of my favorite parts—the part about Paul Revere and the Battle of Bunker Hill.

Totally focused now on the story, I continued to pet Fred and nibble away on my snack.

Wait a minute, I thought. *What snack?* I searched the table for the eggs. Then I remembered I had thrown them away.

I peered down at the food in my hand.

Please let them be chocolate sprinkles, I prayed as I raised my hand slowly.

I brought my hand right up to my eyes.

I stared at the sprinkles between my fingers.

I stared at them as they wiggled their tiny legs.

"Noooo," I moaned. "Oooooh, no! Fleas!"

"I'm eating fleas!" I shrieked.

My stomach heaved.

I clamped my hand over my mouth so I wouldn't throw up—and felt a flea crawl off my finger and across my cheek.

"Aghh!" I swiped it away.

But now something tickled my throat. No, not a tickle. More like a sting.

"Oh, no! There's a flea stuck in my throat!"

I tried to cough it out, but its sharp legs dug in deeper and deeper.

I charged upstairs to the bathroom.

I grabbed my toothbrush and frantically brushed

at my throat. I brushed and brushed until I couldn't feel the flea's pinching legs.

Then I rinsed and watched the flea float down the drain.

Ugh.

I brushed my teeth. I brushed my gums. I brushed my tongue. I brushed the roof of my mouth.

I didn't stop brushing until my entire mouth turned too sore to brush anymore.

I have to tell Kevin. Something is definitely wrong with me. Kevin will help me figure out what it is.

I'll have to tell him about the fleas, I realized. But I knew I didn't have a choice. I needed help — fast.

I dialed the Sullivans' number. Aunt Sylvie answered the phone. "Hello."

"It's Sam Kinny," I said. "Is Kevin there?"

"Hello? Hello?"

"It's Sam Kinny," I repeated. "Is Kevin there?"

"Hello. Who is this? I can't understand you," Aunt Sylvie said.

Must be a bad connection, I thought. "It's Sam Kinny," I shouted into the phone. "Are Kevin or Lissa there?"

"I'm sorry. I still can't understand a word you're saying," she replied. "Concentrate hard—I'll try to read your mind."

I hung up the phone.

I redialed, hoping Kevin would pick up.

"Hello." Aunt Sylvie again.

Maybe she's hard of hearing, I thought.

"It's Sam," I screamed into the phone. "Is Kevin there?"

"Owww!" Aunt Sylvie cried. "Now you've hurt my ears. How rude!" She hung up on me.

Okay. This is it. I'll call once more, then I'm giving up. Aunt Sylvie picked up the phone before the first ring ended.

"It's Sam Kinny," I said. "I didn't mean to hurt your ears, but I was wondering if I could speak to Kevin. It's kind of important."

"Slower! Slower! Please!" Aunt Sylvie said.

Slower?

What did she mean—slower?

"It'sSamKinny," I repeated. "Iwanttospeak with . . ."

Yikes! Aunt Sylvie was right. I was talking fast. Really fast.

I inhaled deeply. I counted to five.

"It'sSamKinny."

Oh, no!

I tried again.

"IhavetospeaktoKevin."

Now *I* couldn't even understand what I was saying.

"I'm not in the mood for jokes, young man," Aunt Sylvie scolded. "Don't call back again." She slammed the phone down with a crash.

"Tsamny! Tsamny!" I repeated the sentence over and over, trying my hardest to slow down. But it didn't work.

I focused on my lips. My tongue. Trying to control them.

"It'sSamKinnyIwanttospeaktoKevinandLissa."

I couldn't slow down no matter how hard I tried.

"It'sSamKinnyIwanttospeakKevandLisIt'sSam KinnyIwanttospeaktoKevandLis."

Oh, no! Now I couldn't stop talking!

I broke out in a cold sweat.

"WtmIgningtdo?" I chattered. "WtmIgningto-do? WtmIgningtdomIgningtodo?"

I grabbed my jaw with both hands and clamped it shut.

I went to my room and stared in the mirror over my dresser.

Very slowly I relaxed the grip on my jaw.

"What."

Before my mouth could utter another word, I clamped my jaw shut with both hands again.

Okay. Stay calm, I told myself. *That was good. You said only one word.*

I relaxed my grip again.

"What."

I said it again. Then clamped my jaw shut.
Then I relaxed it.
"Am."
Clamp. Relax.
"I."
Again.
"Going."
Again.
"To."
One more time.
"Do?"

12

"**W**hat am I going to do?"

"What are you going to do about what, Sam?"

The minute Mom walked through the door, I started to tell her what happened.

I concentrated on speaking slowly, and this time it worked. I was talking like my old self again. I told her about trying to make the phone call and how I couldn't slow down. And how I finally had to hold my jaw shut.

I sat in the kitchen chair, and Mom leaned over me, her brow wrinkled with worry. "When exactly did it start?" she asked.

"About an hour ago," I answered.

"Did it last long?" she asked.

"No, not too long." I shook my head.

"Did you feel hot?" she asked.

I tried to remember if I had felt hot. "No," I said. "I didn't feel hot."

Mom touched my forehead. "Hmmm. Not hot. No fever."

"What do you think is wrong with me?" I asked nervously.

Mom sat down next to me and smiled. "I don't think anything is wrong with you." She patted my hand. "Maybe something you ate disagreed with you. . . ."

Something I ate.

Like paste.

Or fleas.

No way, I told myself. Paste or fleas definitely could not make someone talk that way.

Sponges. What about sponges?

No. They couldn't do it either. It would have to be something weirder than that.

Much weirder . . .

Like those little black flakes, the ones Aunt Sylvie added to my rice pudding.

Those black flakes that burned my mouth and made me feel hot all over!

That's it! I realized.

Aunt Sylvie did this to me.

Why didn't I think of it before?

I remembered what she said after Lissa told her I ate only white food. "You *must* eat more than that," she said.

Then she sneaked those horrible flakes into my dessert. The ones she wouldn't eat. That's when all this crazy stuff started to happen.

A chill ran down my spine.

Aunt Sylvie knows all kinds of weird things about magic spells. Lissa and Kevin told me so.

Those black flakes must be part of a magic spell! An evil magic spell!

I have to talk to Kevin. I'll tell him Aunt Sylvie put some kind of curse on me with those flakes! I have to tell him right away!

I started for the front door, then stopped.

I couldn't go over to Kevin's house. Aunt Sylvie was there—it wasn't safe. And I didn't want to call on the phone again.

I'll wait until tomorrow to talk to him, I decided. I'll tell him at lunch.

The next day in school I watched the clock as the seconds ticked by. The morning seemed to drag on forever. I couldn't concentrate on anything, not even the test on *Johnny Tremaine*. I probably flunked it bigtime. But I didn't care.

All that mattered just then was talking to

Kevin—and figuring out a way to make Aunt Sylvie take this curse off me.

When the lunch bell rang, I jumped up from my seat and grabbed Kevin. "Hurry up! We have to get to the cafeteria fast!"

"All right!" Kevin threw a fist in the air and cheered. "Potato chips, here we come!"

I tried to make Kevin sit right down when we reached the cafeteria, but he insisted on getting his chips first.

I grabbed a seat and waited for him. I opened my lunch, but I couldn't eat. I was way too nervous. I mean, I was about to tell Kevin that his aunt was evil. That she put a curse on me. Wouldn't you be nervous if you had to tell your best friend *that?*

What's taking him so long? I wondered. I searched the food line for him, but I spotted Lissa instead. She waved, then came by and sat down next to me.

Now I'll have to tell them *both* about Aunt Sylvie, I realized. That made me even more nervous.

"How come you're not eating?" Lissa took a big bite out of her peanut butter and jelly sandwich.

"I'm not hungry," I lied as Kevin plopped down next to me with three bags of chips.

"Listen, guys, I have to tell you something really important."

64

Kevin opened the first bag of chips. "Sure, what?" he said, munching away.

Telling Kevin and Lissa this was going to be harder than I thought.

"Well, um, yesterday, after school, something kind of weird happened to me."

"Hey!" Lissa peered up from her peanut butter and jelly sandwich. "Something weird happened to us too."

"It did?" I asked.

Maybe Aunt Sylvie has put some kind of crazy spell on them too. Maybe this was going to be easier than I thought.

"Yeah," Kevin said. "Lissa and I changed after school to go hiking in the woods. When we met downstairs, we were both wearing the same exact thing. Black sweaters, black ripped jeans, and red socks."

"And our jeans were ripped right in the same exact spot. Weird, huh?" Lissa added.

"Um, yeah," I said. "Weird. But something even stranger happened to me. It started a couple of days ago—"

"I need another bag of chips." Kevin jumped up from his seat and headed back to the food line. "Be right back."

I drummed my fingers nervously on the table.

Come on, Kevin. Hurry up. I have to tell you this.

65

We have to figure out what to do before something worse happens.

Kevin returned with another bag of chips. "Okay, what started a couple of days ago?" he asked.

I took a deep breath. Here goes, I thought.

"A couple of days ago, some crazy stuff started happening to me—and it's all because of—"

"Aunt Sylvie!" Lissa yelled.

"Yes!" I cried.

"Hi, Aunt Sylvie!" Lissa waved to someone behind me.

A cold hand gripped my shoulder tightly from behind.

Aunt Sylvie's cold hand.

"Hello, children." Aunt Sylvie smiled warmly at Kevin and Lissa. She shifted her gaze to me—and her eyes narrowed. She stared at me hard.

"Aunt Sylvie, cool dress," Lissa exclaimed.

"Oh, thank you," Aunt Sylvie replied. She spun around to show off the outfit she was wearing. A short neon-green figure-skating dress with a dark purple rhinestone belt and bright purple tights.

Pinned into her gray hair, she wore a sparkly crown—made with the same purple rhinestones as in her belt.

"I was on my way to the ice rink," she explained.

66

"To practice my scratch spin and my double lutz. I do love figure skating!"

"Then how come you're here?" Kevin asked.

Aunt Sylvie dug her fingers deeper into my shoulder. "I have something for Sam." She handed me a brown paper bag with the top folded down. "Something to finish the job."

"Oh, noooo," I moaned.

"What job?" Lissa asked.

"Oh, Sam knows," she replied.

I peered up at Aunt Sylvie.

An eerie smile spread across her lips.

"Open the bag, Sam!" Lissa urged. "I want to see what's inside."

"I'll—I'll open it later," I stammered.

"Aw, come on," Kevin complained. "I don't want to wait until later. Open it now."

"Okay, okay," I groaned.

I set the bag on the table.

I unfolded the top.

Then I peeked inside.

13

"**A**hhhh!" I threw the bag to the floor.

"Very funny." Lissa rolled her eyes.

"Yeah, stop fooling around," Kevin said. "Show us what's inside."

Before I could stop her, Lissa bent down and snapped the bag off the floor.

"Don't look!" I shouted. "You don't want to see what's in there!"

"Sam, calm down." Aunt Sylvie dug her fingers deep into my shoulder. "You seem to be a bit nervous today." Then she laughed at me, mockingly.

Lissa placed the bag on the table. "Let's see—" she said, opening it.

"Don't!" I snatched the bag back. "It's a pair of eyes. *Human eyes!*"

"Oh, don't be silly." Aunt Sylvie chuckled. She grabbed the bag from me. "They're not real eyes at all."

She reached into the bag. "See? Stones. Beautiful midnight-blue stones."

"What are they for?" Kevin asked.

"They're for Sam's mother," Aunt Sylvie replied. "I met her in the crafts store yesterday. She told me she was searching for blue eyes for a doll she's making—"

"Sam's mother makes really cool dolls," Lissa interrupted.

"Yes. That's what the owner of the crafts store said too. Well, I told Sam's mother to search no further! I had the most beautiful blue stones from my last trip to Borneo. Perfect for eyes. And here they are!"

Aunt Sylvie handed the bag back to me.

I took it from her with a trembling hand.

"Sam, are you okay? Why is your hand shaking like that?" Aunt Sylvie asked.

"I—I haven't been feeling very well," I told her. "Since the night I ate the rice pudding."

Aunt Sylvie leaned close to me.

She lowered her face to mine.

She stared deep into my eyes. Stared and stared, as if she were searching for something.

"Ah-ha! There it is," she whispered. "I knew it would be!"

14

"**W**hat?" What's there?" I leaped up from my seat.

"Sit!" She pushed me down.

She placed her hands on top of my head and began making circles with her fingers. Small ones at first, then larger ones.

"Ooooom," she chanted deeply as she pressed her fingers into my skull. "Ooooma, ooooma, ooooma."

"What did you see, Aunt Sylvie?" Lissa asked. "What did you see in Sam's eyes?"

"Too much yin. Not enough yang," she replied.

"What's that?" Kevin asked.

"Yin is everything that is dark, cold, and wet in nature.

"Yang is everything that is light, warm, and dry," she tried to explain to us.

"I learned all about it when I visited China. Sam has too much yin. He's off balance. Not to worry though. I think I've cured him. I learned this technique from an old Chinese witch doctor."

"A witch doctor!" I jerked away.

Aunt Sylvie circled my head one last time. "Oh, my!" She glanced up at the clock. "I'm going to be late for my skating lesson."

I watched Aunt Sylvie head out the cafeteria door.

Why didn't she stop by my house and give the doll eyes to my mother?

Why did she give them to me in school?

Weird, I thought. Really weird.

I had to tell Kevin and Lissa about Aunt Sylvie now!

"Something is wrong with me," I started to say. "Something terrible."

Kevin and Lissa stared at me, waiting for me to go on.

I picked up the pepper shaker from the table and unscrewed the lid. "You're not going to believe me," I went on. "But you have to."

Kevin and Lissa nodded.

72

I poured some pepper into my hand.

"It started the night I ate dinner at your house."

"Sam, what are you doing?" Lissa glanced down at my palm.

I lifted my hand to my mouth.

I lapped up the pepper in my hand.

"Sam! That's disgusting!" Lissa yelled.

I brought the shaker up to my mouth and began pouring the pepper down my throat.

"SAM! Stop!" Kevin ordered.

I wanted to stop.

I tried to stop.

But I couldn't. I couldn't stop no matter how hard I tried.

Kevin reached across the table and snatched the shaker from my lips. Pepper spilled everywhere.

"Give that back to me!" I yelled, trying to grab it from him.

I had to have that pepper.

Kevin held it out of my reach.

I lowered my head and licked the spilled pepper off the table.

"SAM!" Lissa shrieked. "STOP!"

"I want to stop, But I can't!" I yelled. "That's what I've been trying to tell you."

"Why can't you stop?" Lissa demanded.

"Because I'm a little excited." *Why did I say that? I didn't mean to say that. Did I?*

73

The pepper burned my throat. I swigged some milk from my container.

"I need your help! You're the only ones who can help me."

"We'll help you," Kevin said. "But you have to tell us what's wrong."

"I know I've been acting kind of crazy, and it's all because I'm under a—"

"Under a what?" Lissa asked impatiently.

"What?" Kevin echoed.

"I'm under a chow chow poodle German shepherd."

Huh?

Why did I say *that*?

I definitely didn't want to say that!

Kevin and Lissa laughed.

"I'm under a terrier Lassie boxer Pekingese," I declared.

Oh, no! What's going on? I know what I want to say! Why are all the wrong words coming out?

The lunch period warning bell rang.

"We have to go, Sam." Kevin and Lissa stood up.

Tell them! Tell them about the dog food and the fleas!

My heart began to race.

I opened my mouth.

Would the right words come out?

74

I concentrated on what I wanted to say—and shouted, "Rin-Tin-Tin!"

Kevin and Lissa gathered up their books.

"Pit bull!" I cried out.

Why couldn't I say what I meant?

I had to tell them how Aunt Sylvie put a curse on me with those little black flakes.

That's it! I gasped.

That's why she came to school!

She knows I've figured out she's the one doing this to me.

And she doesn't want me to tell Kevin and Lissa!

So she came to school and sang that weird chant over my head—to strengthen the curse.

To make sure I'd never be able to tell anyone about it—ever!

15

"**D**oberman beagle Newfoundland," I screamed, trying to tell them about Aunt Sylvie. "Labrador schnauzer Lhasa apso!"

"Sam," Lissa said. "Why are you doing this?"

"I'm trying to tell you why!" I shouted. But all that came out was "Schnauzer mutt Greyhound!"

"Stop it!" Lissa shook her head impatiently.

"Collie retriever—"

"Sam, stop it. I mean it!" Lissa reached over and socked me in the arm hard.

"Owww!" I yelled. "That really hurt!"

"I'm sorry," Lissa apologized. "But I had to make you stop."

"You didn't have to hit me so hard," I said, rubbing my arm. "You could have broken something."

Hey! I'm talking!

"Okay, quit joking around now," Kevin said, "and tell us what you wanted to say."

"I wasn't joking around," I protested. "It's part of the curse."

"What curse?" Kevin asked.

"The curse your Aunt Sylvie put on me!" I cried.

"Sam, you really are crazy!" Lissa shrieked.

"No, I'm not!"

I told Kevin and Lissa about eating the sponges. I reminded Kevin about the paste and the weird shocks. I told them how I wanted to eat Fred's dog food.

I told them about talking so fast yesterday, I couldn't even understand myself.

I told them that I ate fleas.

"And it all started after Aunt Sylvie put those black flakes in my rice pudding," I finished. "I was fine before that. Perfectly fine."

"Fleas! You ate fleas!" Lissa gagged. "That's disgusting."

"But we all ate the rice pudding," Kevin said. "Nothing weird happened to us."

"No, you didn't," I reminded him. "I was the only one who tasted the rice pudding. Then Aunt

Sylvie poured the black flakes down the drain. Remember—she wouldn't even taste them. She just threw them out. Then everyone ate ice cream."

"Why would Aunt Sylvie put a curse on you?" Kevin demanded.

"Because she doesn't like picky eaters!" I exclaimed.

"That's ridiculous," Lissa declared.

"Then how would *you* explain what's been happening to me?" I asked.

"I don't know, but it's not Aunt Sylvie's fault," she replied.

"It is!" I insisted, totally frustrated. "Aunt Sylvie put a curse on me. You've got to believe me." I banged my hand on the table hard.

"Look, Sam. You cut yourself," Kevin said, gazing down at my hand.

"I don't care about my hand!" I shouted. "I'm under a curse!"

"Look at your hand, Sam!" Kevin exclaimed.

"Look!" Lissa said, her eyes growing wider and wider.

I gazed down at my hand.

Blood oozed from the cut and dripped onto the table.

A thick stream of blood.

Bright blue blood.

16

"**B**lue blood!" I shrieked. "I have blue blood!"

"Is—is it real?" Lissa stammered.

"Of course it's real!" I shouted. I grabbed a napkin from the table and pressed it to my hand. The napkin soaked up the blood and turned bright blue instantly.

"Why—why is it blue?" she asked.

"I don't know why it's blue," I cried. "Something made it blue—or someone."

I lifted the napkin from my hand and a thick stream of blue blood squirted from the cut. It splattered all over Lissa's light yellow T-shirt.

"Ewww!" She jumped back. "Wipe it off me!"

Kevin grabbed a napkin and tried to blot the blood from Lissa's shirt.

"Now do you believe me?" I asked. "Something weird is going on. Something really weird! And it started after I ate those black flakes."

"I can't believe this is Aunt Sylvie's fault," Lissa argued. "She would never hurt anyone."

Kevin agreed. "But I bet she can figure out what's wrong with you," he said. "She knows all kinds of cool things."

Right, I thought. Like how to poison someone.

I glanced down at my hand. Fresh blood dripped from the cut. Fresh blue blood.

"I'm going home!" I told them. "I have to find my parents and tell them what's been going on. I have to tell them before it's too late."

I wrapped another napkin around the cut and ran all the way home.

"Mom! Mom!" I called from the front door. "Come quick."

Fred trotted over to greet me. He sniffed at my bandaged hand and backed away.

"Mom! Where are you? I need you."

My mother wasn't home.

I raced into the kitchen to find Dad's telephone number at work. I called his office, but the man who answered the phone said Dad was out to lunch.

What am I going to do now?

I don't know where Mom is. Or when she'll be back. I can't wait for Dad to come back from lunch—I don't know how long someone can live with blue blood.

A doctor! That's it—I'll call a doctor.

I searched through Mom's phone book.

I skimmed every single page.

But I couldn't find the name of a single doctor—except for Dr. Stone, Fred's veterinarian.

Should I go to the vet?

Yes. I had no other choice.

I dashed out of the house and ran right into Kevin and Lissa.

"What are you doing here?" I asked.

"We came to help you," Kevin said. "Where are you going?"

"I'm going to see Dr. Stone," I said.

"Where's Fred?" Lissa asked, searching for Fred.

"I'm—I'm not taking Fred. I'm going for—me."

"You're going to a veterinarian!" Lissa cried. "That's ridiculous."

"I don't know what else to do!" I shouted. "Mom's not home. Dad's at lunch. I can't find the name of a regular doctor. And my blood is still blue!" I held up my hand and showed them the dried blue blood.

"No way!" Kevin protested. "You are not going to a vet. You are coming with us."

"I am *not* going home with you!" I declared.

"Something *is* wrong with you, Sam," Lissa said. "And Aunt Sylvie will know what to do."

"She's done enough!" I yelled.

"What if we sneak into her room and search through her stuff. See if we can find anything about a black-flake curse," Kevin suggested, rolling his eyes.

I thought about that for a moment.

Maybe that made sense.

Maybe we could find a cure in her room for the curse.

Dr. Stone probably wouldn't know anything about the black-flake curse.

"Okay." I gave in. "But I don't want her to know I'm there. We have to sneak into the house."

Kevin and Lissa agreed.

As we walked along Fear Street, I noticed a tall maple tree a few houses from the corner—in the Knowltons' front yard.

I'd never seen such a tall tree before. Its branches towered over all the houses around it.

"How long has that tree been there?" I asked.

"Probably about a million years," Lissa said.

I stared up at the tree. At its red and gold leaves

as they floated to the ground. "I wonder why I never noticed it before."

"Why would anyone notice a maple tree?" Kevin said. "They all look alike."

"How could you miss that tree?" Lissa declared. "It must be thirty feet tall."

I stopped at the Knowltons' gate. I pushed it open and walked into their front yard. I gazed down at the ground.

"Sam, what are you staring at?" Kevin asked.

"The leaves," I replied. "They look so delicious."

I sank to my knees—and began stuffing the red and gold leaves into my mouth.

I grabbed handful after handful from the ground. I stuffed my mouth full with leaves. They tasted drier than sand, but I couldn't stop.

"Sam!" Kevin shouted. "Get up!"

"We have to stop him, Kevin," Lissa wailed. "We have to do something!"

Kevin and Lissa each grabbed one of my arms. They tried to tug me away from the leaves.

"Let me go!" I shouted. "I have to eat these leaves!"

Lissa grabbed my head in one of her karate holds and yanked me back.

"Please, just one more leaf," I begged. "Just one more."

"Don't believe him, Lissa," Kevin shouted. "I've seen him eat paste. Once he starts, he can't stop. If you let him go, he'll eat every tree on Fear Street!"

Lissa and Kevin dragged me back to the sidewalk.

I took a deep breath.

"Thanks. I'm okay now," I told them.

"Boy, you really do need help," Lissa said, shaking her head. "That was disgusting, Sam. Really disgusting."

I picked a leaf out from between my teeth. "I know," I moaned.

We walked a few steps—right by my front door.

I thought about Aunt Sylvie.

About her mocking laugh. Her evil chant.

I decided to go home.

"Oh, no, you don't." Kevin pulled me back. "We're going to my house, remember?"

Kevin tugged me past my house. We walked by Mrs. Kowalski's front lawn—and I took a dive. Right into her flower garden.

"Sam, please. No more leaves!" Lissa cried.

Not leaves, Lissa. Dirt. Dark, rich, wet dirt.

I threw myself to the ground.

I didn't even bother scooping up the dirt with my hands.

I lowered my head to the ground—and licked it up with my tongue.

Delicious dirt.

"Oh, noooo," I heard Lissa moan.

I paid no attention.

I buried my head in the dirt and lapped it up.

My eye caught a chrysanthemum. A pretty yellow mum. I snapped its stalk and shoved the flower into my mouth.

And then I spotted a worm. A big, juicy worm.

I opened my mouth and dangled it over my waiting tongue.

I dropped it in. I felt its slimy body slither across my teeth.

I bit into it.

Mmmmm. So moist. So tasty.

I reached down into the soil for another one— and everything went black.

17

"**H**ey! What's going on?" I cried, kicking my arms and legs.

"Hold still, Sam," Lissa demanded. "It's just my jacket over your head. It's the only way we could get you to stop."

I touched the top of my head, feeling for Lissa's jacket. Yes, that's what it was. She was telling the truth.

Kevin and Lissa guided me down the sidewalk, block after block, with Lissa's jacket over my head.

"Are you okay in there, Sam?" Lissa asked.

"No. I am not okay. Take this thing off my head! Now!"

"I don't think we should, Sam," Kevin said. "If we do, we'll lose control over you. Sorry."

I guess I couldn't blame them.

"It's okay," I said. "Anyway, with this jacket over my head I don't feel like eating dirt anymore. I guess if I can't see it, I don't want to eat it."

I couldn't wait to get to the Sullivans' house. I needed a drink of water badly—to wash away the horrible, sour-worm-juice taste in my mouth.

Worm juice.

Ugh.

I can't believe I bit into a worm.

We have to find a clue in Aunt Sylvie's room, I prayed. *We have to!*

"Okay, Sam!" Lissa whisked the jacket from my head. I blinked in the bright light of the Sullivans' hallway.

I caught my reflection in the hall mirror. My hair was matted with mud. Dirt streaked across my cheeks, my nose, my lips. What a mess!

"Anybody home?" Kevin called out.

"What are you doing?" I clamped my dirty hand over his mouth. "I told you—I don't want Aunt Sylvie to know I'm here."

Kevin yanked my hand away. "Hey, relax. I just wanted to make sure she was gone, that's all."

87

Aunt Sylvie didn't answer.

No one did.

"Come on." Kevin motioned us toward the steps. "Let's go up to Aunt Sylvie's room."

Aunt Sylvie's room was exactly as I remembered it. The mat where she slept rested in the middle of the floor. The ancient wooden medicine mask and the Indian dream catcher still hung on the wall. Crystals in every hue and tint lined the dresser.

"Where should we look first?" I asked.

"The books," Kevin suggested. "Maybe that's where we'll find out what happened to you."

I gazed around the room. "I don't see any books."

"In here," Kevin said, opening the door to Aunt Sylvie's closet.

Kevin snapped on the closet light. Rows and rows of bookshelves lined the closet walls.

I grabbed a few books from a shelf. "Come on, let's start reading." I handed one book to Kevin and one to Lissa. "Maybe we can find the black-flake curse in one of these."

Kevin read the title of his book. *"You Don't Have to Whisper—How to Talk to the Dead."*

Then Lissa read hers. *"Herbs and Berries."*

Mine said *The Magic of Spices.* "Hey! I bet I can find out what's wrong with me in this one!" I exclaimed.

I eagerly flipped through the pages. But all I found were recipes for one kind of ailment or another. Nagging backache, clogged sinuses, hacking cough. You name it, this book had a cure for it.

I knew I wouldn't find what I was looking for in there. The book explained how to make people better—not what made people sick.

Kevin and Lissa searched through the bookshelves. "Do you see any books on poisons?" I asked.

"Not yet," Lissa called out.

"Well, keep looking!" I pleaded.

I wandered around the room searching for a clue.

I gazed up at the wooden mask.

A medicine mask from an ancient mountain tribe.

I remembered what Kevin and Lissa had told me about it. They said it was supposed to drive germs right out of a sick person's body.

But how did it work? Did the sick person wear it? Or did a witch doctor have to wear it and say some weird chant?

I didn't know—but I decided to try it. Maybe it could help me.

I carefully lifted the mask from the wall.

I slipped it over my face—and waited.

I could see out of the eyeholes. And I was breathing through a hole for the mouth.

I didn't feel any different.

With the mask over my face, I continued to roam around the room. I ran my fingers over the dream catcher's feathers, over Aunt Sylvie's crystals, over a jar of face cream that sat on the dresser.

I unscrewed the lid and dipped my fingers into the pure white cream. Then I licked my fingers.

Mmmm. So smooth. So good.

I scooped out a bigger glob and ate that.

"Ahhhh!" Lissa screamed.

Kevin whirled around to face me. "It's just Sam wearing a mask, Lissa. Get a grip."

"It's not the mask, you jerk," she yelled. "He's eating Aunt Sylvie's face cream."

Lissa and Kevin threw the coat over my head. "Let's get him out of here before he finishes the jar," Kevin said.

They dragged me from Aunt Sylvie's room. They pulled me along the hall and down the stairs. When they reached the kitchen, they let me go.

I threw the coat off.

"Aunt Sylvie's going to be mad now," Kevin said. "Very mad."

"Yeah," Lissa agreed. "That cream is two hundred years old. She told us it contains ancient powers for long-lasting beauty. And it was her last jar."

"Her only jar," Kevin corrected his sister.

"How can you worry about her jar of face

cream?" I yelled. "Your aunt is evil. She put a curse on me!"

But Lissa wasn't listening. She gazed over my shoulder—at something out the back door.

I turned and scanned the garden.

Flowers, trees, shrubs, a wooden bench.

Then I saw her. Aunt Sylvie.

Lissa grabbed my hand. "You have to tell Aunt Sylvie what's going on. She can help you!" she pleaded.

"NO!" I declared. "Never."

Lissa and Kevin dragged me out the back door—and I gasped.

Aunt Sylvie sat on the ground, cross-legged, with her eyes closed.

Six black snakes slithered around her neck, her arms, her legs.

I watched in horror as they twisted along her body, their long, pointed tongues darting in and out.

Aunt Sylvie swayed back and forth, in a deep trance.

"Ondu . . . ondu . . . ondu," she chanted.

She waved her hands over a big iron kettle that bubbled over with a dark brown liquid.

Then she lifted a wooden mask from the ground. A mask with black lips twisted into a sickening leer. She placed it over her face.

"She's a witch doctor!" I cried.

"Aunt—Aunt Sylvie," Lissa stammered. "Are you a witch doctor?"

Aunt Sylvie slowly removed the mask from her face.

Her eyes fluttered open.

She leveled a steady gaze at us.

"Yes, dear, I am."

18

~~~

Aunt Sylvie slowly rose to her feet—as though some strange power we couldn't see lifted her up. Singing softly to her snakes, she swayed back and forth on her heels.

The snakes around her arms slithered across her body.

Aunt Sylvie gently stroked them. "Odru kan toka," she crooned to them.

The snake around her neck waved its head in the air. Its tongue darted in and out. Aunt Sylvie kissed the top of its head.

"Odum ruba kantan," she chanted softly. "Odum ruba kantan haroo."

"Wh-what are you saying?" Lissa stammered.

"Shhhh!" Aunt Sylvie whispered, placing a finger on her lips. "You'll break the spell."

Aunt Sylvie carefully unwrapped the snakes from her arms and legs and set them down in a tank behind her. The snake around her neck remained coiled around her neck.

"Okay, children." She turned toward us. "Now you can ask your questions."

"Wh-what language were you speaking?" Kevin asked.

"The language of all witch doctors." Aunt Sylvie smiled and kissed the snake on the top of its head once more.

Then she moved toward me slowly.

"Sam, would you like to meet Rabia Wan?" she asked, petting the snake. "I don't believe you've met her yet."

Aunt Sylvie walked closer to me. Closer. Until she stood only inches away.

The she grabbed the snake—and thrust it into my face. Its fanged tongue darted out, barely missing my cheek.

I leaped away and screamed.

"I see you're still a bit nervous, Sam." Aunt Sylvie laughed. "Are your hands still shaking? Perhaps I need to say another chant."

"Don't touch me!" I backed away. "Don't come near me!"

"Are you really a witch doctor?" Lissa asked.

"Of course I'm not a witch doctor." Aunt Sylvie laughed louder this time. "But the tribe I lived with in Brazil thought I was. They loved my snake-charming act. Too bad Sam doesn't. Sorry if I frightened you, Sam."

"That's just an act?" Kevin asked. "It's not real?"

"Oh, anyone can learn how to do it." Aunt Sylvie dropped the snake around her neck into the tank. "The most wonderful snake charmer in Ceylon taught me—with these six little beauties. They're perfectly harmless."

"See, Sam!" Kevin turned toward me. "Aunt Sylvie is *not* a witch doctor. She did *not* put a curse on you!"

"Sam!" Aunt Sylvie exclaimed. "Did you really think I put a curse on you? How could you have imagined such a thing?"

"You—you did put a curse on me," I choked out. "I know it! You put a horrible curse on me with those little black flakes."

"Little black flakes?" Aunt Sylvie pretended she didn't know what I was talking about.

"Yes! The black flakes you hid in my rice pudding!" I told her. "Ever since I ate them, I can't eat white food anymore. It tastes terrible. Everything tastes terrible to me—except worms and fleas and dirt—"

"Sam," Aunt Sylvie interrupted, "why would I want you to eat dirt?"

"Because you're crazy—because you don't like picky eaters!" I shouted.

"That's nonsense!" Aunt Sylvie shook her head. "But maybe I know a cure for this. Let me think. Let me think."

"Stay away from me!" I yelled. "I know what you're going to do. You're going to say another one of your evil chants so I won't be able to speak. So I won't be able to tell anyone what you did to me!"

Aunt Sylvie shook her head. "Poor Sam," she said. "You can speak all you want, dear. I'm afraid no one could possibly believe a word you're saying."

"Can you help Sam?" Lissa asked Aunt Sylvie. "Do you have any idea what's wrong with him?"

"Well, he might have an allergy. I've seen allergies cause very odd symptoms. Or perhaps he's suffering from a virus." Aunt Sylvie turned to me. "You really should see a doctor, Sam. It's not wise to let this continue any longer. Who knows what could happen next?"

I ran from the Sullivans' house. I ran as fast as I could—before Aunt Sylvie could cast any more of her evil magic.

As I raced around the corner to my block, I slowed down.

I had to.

Something was wrong with my feet—they tingled all over. I walked a few steps—and felt the tingling in my hands too.

I stared down at my fingers—and gasped.

My fingers were swelling. I watched in horror as they grew wider and wider.

I walked faster now.

The tingling spread to my wrists and arms.

My arms began to bulge larger and larger.

They strained against my shirt.

I heard a loud rip as they tore through my sleeves—tore them to shreds.

"Help!" I cried out. "Someone, help me! It's spreading. The curse is spreading!"

19

~~~

I crawled toward my front door.

The seams of my pants and sneakers split against the weight of my legs and feet. My enormous legs and feet.

"Mom! Dad! Help me, please!" I collapsed at the front door, gasping for breath.

Dad's car pulled into the driveway. As soon as he saw me, he jumped out of the car and rushed to my side.

"Dad, something's wrong with me," I groaned. "My arms . . . my legs . . . I'm going to explode!"

Dad studied my hands and feet. His forehead wrinkled with worry. "Don't worry, Sam." He helped me up and brought me into the living room. "Everything's going to be okay."

"It's not going to be okay," I said. "You don't understand. I've been doing all kinds of weird stuff. And eating all kinds of crazy things."

"What do you mean, Sam? What did you eat?"

"Sponges and leaves and glue and dirt and worms," I told him.

"Sam!" Mom came through the front door and gaped at my swollen body. "What's wrong? What's wrong with Sam?" she asked my father.

"I'm 'bout to splode!" I exclaimed.

Mom shook her head. "You're about to *what*, Sam?"

I tried to tell her I was about to explode. But my tongue blew up. It filled my entire mouth now.

Dad carried me down the hall and into the kitchen. Mom followed right behind him.

"Poor Sam is scared to death," Dad said to her.

"What's wong wit me?" I asked, banging my swollen arms against the hall wall.

Dad sat me in a kitchen chair.

"Wook!" I cried. The cut in my hand had opened up. "Bwoo bwuud! I have bwoo bwuud!"

"Oh, look." Mom sighed. "He's cut himself. He's bleeding too."

Dad examined my hand.

"Bwooo!" I shrieked. "Bwooo bwuud!"

"Calm down, Sam." Dad patted my head. "I can fix you right up. I know just what to do. Let's go down to the basement."

Dad knows what to do?

How does he know what to do? Does he know how to break a curse?

I tried to ask, but I couldn't speak anymore. My tongue hung out of my mouth, totally red and swollen.

"I bet he ate something strange . . ." Dad started to say.

Yes! I nodded my head furiously. That's it! That's it!

"Something spicy," he continued. "It must have short-circuited his digestive system. Probably gave him those cravings for nonfoods."

Short circuits! What is dad talking about?

My father lifted me up and sat me on his workbench. "A few new chips and he'll be as good as new!"

A few new chips!

What is going on here?

Dad slipped his toolbox off a shelf. "While I'm at it, I'll adjust his digestive system."

I watched in terror as he selected a large screwdriver from his toolbox and approached me.

What is he going to do to me?

My mother shook her head. "I should have been

paying closer attention," she said. "I should have realized what was happening when he told me he was having trouble speaking."

"Oh, don't blame yourself," Dad said. "These glitches happen."

Glitches!

I turned to Mom, my eyes wide with fear. *What is he talking about?* I tried to scream. No words came out.

"But he was so upset." Mom sighed.

"He'll be as good as new in no time," Dad assured her. "The more weird things he ate, the more damage he did to everything—his motor skills, language skills, everything."

"That must explain the swelling too, I suppose," Mom said.

What are they talking about?

"Oh, absolutely," Dad agreed. "But I'm going to give him a new digestive system so this won't happen again."

Dad moved in closer to me.

He smiled at Mom. "He'll be fine," he said. "Your favorite doll will be back to normal before his bedtime!"

20

"**I** am not going to wear that stupid Pilgrim hat," Kevin complained to me at lunch a few weeks later.

"You have to wear the hat," I said, taking a bite of my lunch. "Or you'll hurt Ms. Munson's feelings. Besides, you won't be the only one who looks stupid. We all have to wear them."

"I guess." Kevin shrugged his shoulders.

"Hi, guys!" Lissa sat down next to us. "Hey, that's your fourth bag of chips." She pointed to the three empty bags on the table. "If you eat any more, you're going to explode."

"No, I won't," Kevin said. "I threw out my sandwich. I'm eating only chips for lunch today."

Lissa unwrapped her peanut butter and jelly sandwich and took a big bite. "How are you feeling, Sam? You seem a lot better."

"I am," I said. "I feel much better. Aunt Sylvie was right. I must have had a virus or something."

"What's that in your sandwich?" Lissa asked, leaning over the table.

"Meatballs," I answered, "with ketchup on rye bread."

"You're eating meatballs?" Lissa's eyebrows shot up. "With ketchup on rye bread?"

"Sure," I said. "What's the big deal? I'm not the one who has to eat peanut butter and jelly for lunch every single day. I'm like Kevin—just a normal kid."

Are you ready for another walk
down Fear Street?
Turn the page for a terrifying
sneak preview.

R·L·STINE'S

GHOSTS of FEAR STREET ® #12

NIGHT OF THE WERECAT

Coming mid-August 1996

Wendy reached out and gently touched the Persian cat's back. Its long white fur was as soft as a silk scarf.

"She likes you," Mrs. Bast commented.

"All cats like Wendy," Tina said.

"And I like all cats," Wendy added. She scratched Samantha under the chin. The white cat began to purr. It was Wendy's favorite sound.

Mrs. Bast rubbed her hands together. "What are you looking for today?" she asked. "Jewelry? Photos? T-shirts? Knick-knacks? I've got them all!"

Wendy turned her attention from Samantha to the shelves and displays in the booth. There were trays of cat pins, earrings, bracelets, and necklaces. T-shirts hung from a rack. A clothesline across the top of the booth held posters of lions, tigers, cheetahs, and panthers.

"This is pretty," Tina remarked. She held up a purple bracelet made of cat-shaped beads.

Wendy poked through a tray on the counter labeled "All items $5." A shiny object caught her eye. "Tina, look!" she exclaimed. She held up a silver chain. A delicate metal charm of a black cat dangled in front of her eyes. In the center of the cat's forehead was a spidery white star.

Tina turned to see the necklace. "It's pretty," Tina agreed. "But what's that weird white spot on its face?"

"That's what I like best about it," Wendy said. She ran her finger lightly over the white mark. It was so unusual. And the cat looked so real! "I'm going to take this," Wendy told Mrs. Bast. She held out the charm.

The old woman glanced at the trinket and gave a startled gasp. Then she scowled. "That charm isn't for sale," she snapped. In a quick move, Mrs. Bast snatched the necklace from Wendy's hand.

Wendy was shocked. "But why not?" she blurted. "It was in the tray with all the other cat charms."

"It's not for sale," Mrs. Bast repeated. "And it's not a cat charm. It's a *werecat* charm. That white star on its face is the mark of the werecat."

Werecat? Wendy glanced at Tina. Tina raised her eyebrows.

"What's a werecat?" Tina asked.

"Have you heard of werewolves?" Mrs. Bast demanded.

"Everyone's heard of werewolves," Wendy replied. "They're people who supposedly turn into wolves when the moon is full."

"Werecats are the same," Mrs. Bast said. "Only they turn into cats. Very large, very wild cats. And they do it every night, whether the moon is full or not."

Tina snorted. "But werewolves aren't real," she protested.

"I don't know about werewolves," the old woman said. "But werecats are very real indeed." She poked her head out of the booth and glanced around. Seeming satisfied that no one was listening, Mrs. Bast continued. "I've seen them myself," she whispered. "Right here in Shadyside. They prowl the Fear Street Woods."

Wendy looked at Tina and they both smiled. They loved stories about Fear Street.

Everyone told stories about the creepy things that happened there. But Wendy had been in the Fear Street Woods lots of times. And except for twisting her ankle once when she tripped, nothing terrifying ever happened to her! Still, she and Tina loved to hear all the Fear Street rumors.

"After midnight," Mrs. Bast continued in her croaking voice, "that's when the werecats roam."

"Like alley cats?" Wendy asked.

Mrs. Bast shook her head. "Not at all. You would never mistake a werecat for an ordinary alley cat. A werecat is more daring. All its senses are sharper. It can see, smell, and hunt better. Even its balance is better than a regular cat's. Werecats are beautiful, fierce creatures."

"My cat, Shalimar, is fierce when I don't feed him." Tina giggled. "Maybe he's really a werecat!"

"Maybe we should bring Shalimar over to the Fear Street Woods!" Wendy joked.

"Hah!" Mrs. Bast's barking laugh made Wendy jump. "A werecat would attack your Shalimar if he got in its way. Werecats and regular cats are mortal enemies."

"Shal can take care of himself," Tina insisted.

"He wouldn't stand a chance with a werecat," Mrs. Bast replied. "They run on pure instinct, and they are very powerful. And just like an ordinary cat, werecats are territorial. A werecat will defend its home to the death."

"Why do they only appear after midnight?" Wendy asked. She didn't believe a word Mrs. Bast said, but she liked any story about cats. Especially one that included Fear Street.

"All cats are nocturnal," Mrs. Bast explained. Her voice dropped to a whisper. "But late night is the time of the werecat. And as the moon grows fuller, the werecat grows wilder. There's no way to predict what it will do."

"But if they turn back into people by day, don't they think like humans?" Wendy demanded.

"During most of the month, there is a bit of the

human left in a werecat," Mrs. Bast agreed. "But when the moon is full, the human no longer has any control over the animal. And once the werecat experiences its first full moon, the transformation is complete."

"What do you mean?" Wendy asked.

"After that first full moon, the werecat inside begins to do things—even in human form. Even during the day. The human and the cat blend together."

Mrs. Bast fell silent. Wendy thought the story was over. She glanced at Tina, and Tina rolled her eyes. She obviously thought Mrs. Bast was nuts.

But now Wendy wanted the cat charm even more. "What a cool story!" she told Mrs. Bast. "Please, I have to buy the charm now. It will be my favorite cat jewelry!" She held out a five-dollar bill.

"No!" Mrs. Bast snapped. "I can not allow you to have it. It wouldn't be right!"

Wendy stared at the old woman. What was Mrs. Bast's problem?

"Come on, Wendy," Tina murmured. She tugged Wendy's sleeve. "Let's go look at some more cats."

But Wendy wouldn't give up. She wanted the charm!

"Please, Mrs. Bast—" she began again. But before she could say anything else, the white cat leaped off the counter and slipped under the curtain.

The old woman gasped. "Samantha! Come back here!" She dropped the werecat charm and hurried after the cat. Tina followed her out of the booth.

Wendy's heart stopped. The beautiful charm lay on the table. Right in front of her hand.

I found it in the five-dollar tray, Wendy told herself. There was no reason why she shouldn't have it. Besides, it wasn't like she was *stealing.* She would pay for it.

Wendy could hear Mrs. Bast and Tina moving behind the booth.

"Samantha," Mrs. Bast crooned. "Here sweetie."

Her hand shaking, Wendy slowly placed the five-dollar bill on the tray. Then she grabbed the necklace and looped it around her neck. She quickly fastened it and slipped it inside her T-shirt.

She did it! She couldn't believe she actually did it! Her heart pounded in her chest. She felt a strange tingling sensation where the charm touched her skin.

"Tina!" Wendy called. "Let's go!" She wanted to get out of the booth before Mrs. Bast noticed the charm was gone. *But I didn't steal it,* she told herself again.

Tina popped her head into the booth. "Let's get back to the show," Wendy said.

Tina looked puzzled. "But—"

Wendy quickly interrupted her. "Isn't it time to meet your mom?"

Tina glanced at her watch. "Ooops," she said. "You're right."

"Got to go, Mrs. Bast!" Wendy called over her shoulder. She and Tina hurried back to the main hall.

Wendy stepped into the huge room, then stopped in surprise. The moment she entered the room, she heard a horrifying sound. She and Tina stood still.

A terrible wailing filled the air. Wendy shuddered. Her entire body tensed.

The sound grew louder and weirder.

A chill ran up Wendy's spine and she clapped her hands over her ears. She couldn't stand it.

It was the most terrifying sound she had ever heard.

The screeching sound grew. Louder. Louder. Wendy searched the room, frantically trying to find out where the sound came from. Then her mouth dropped open in surprise.

The horrible wailing came from the caged cats!

"What's wrong with them?" Wendy cried.

"I don't know," Tina shouted over the noise. "But it's awful! Let's get out of here."

They ran through the exhibits, their hands covering their ears. But they could still hear the terrible sound. They raced by table after table of screeching cats. As Wendy passed Cyril's cage, a furry paw reached out and clawed her.

The moment they stepped through the exit, Wendy heard something even stranger. Silence. The yowling stopped.

Tina and Wendy slowly lowered their hands. They stared at each other for a moment.

"That was totally weird," Tina finally said.

"Totally," Wendy agreed. *What could have made the cats act like that?* she wondered.

Standing at her mirror that night, Wendy pulled the cat necklace out from under her shirt. She stroked the cool metal. *I wish it were real,* Wendy thought. *I wish I really had a cat.*

She changed into her nightgown and crawled into bed. She patted the charm again. She thought of all the beautiful cats she had seen that day. Cats that would never be hers.

At least I can dream about them, she thought as she fell asleep.

Later that night, Wendy woke up suddenly. A bright light shone through the window. She glanced at her bedside clock and noticed that it was one minute to midnight.

What was that light? Wendy got up and peered

through the window. She could see the moon rising through the old oak tree in the side yard.

Weird, she thought. The moonlight never woke her up before. Was it always that bright? She started to climb back into bed when she felt a warm spot on her chest. She glanced down. The cat charm seemed to be glowing with a greenish inner light.

She held it between her fingers, trying to get a better look at the glowing light. Her fingertips tingled where she touched the charm.

What is going on? Wendy wondered.

The tingling spread. From her fingers into her hands and up her arms. A strange itchy feeling moved down her back and chest, covering her whole body. She felt warm all over.

I must be getting sick, she told herself. *That's it. I'm sick.*

But this didn't feel like any flu or cold she had ever had before. Besides, Wendy didn't feel sick, exactly. Just . . . peculiar. Then her fingertips began to ache. *What would make that happen?* she wondered.

All ten of her fingers throbbed now. Her fingernails actually hurt. Puzzled, she held them up to her face.

In the bright moonlight she could see that her

fingernails were very long, much longer than she remembered them. How could they have grown so fast?

Wendy's heart began to beat faster. *What's happening to me?*

She took a closer look at her hands.

Fear rose in her throat. Fear so strong it almost choked her.

Sprouting from the tips of her fingers weren't fingernails.

They were long, sharp, curved claws.

"No! Wendy whispered in horror.

Wendy couldn't tear her eyes away. She could see the claws grow longer. Her fingers started to shrink—becoming shorter and thicker. Wendy's stomach churned as she watched long, reddish-blond hair sprout on the backs of her hands.

She tried to move her fingers but couldn't. They had fused together. Her hands looked exactly like paws!

Her whole body itched. She glanced down. Fur was growing on her arms, her legs, her chest. Everywhere!

Her ears tickled. She reached up with her furry paws to touch them. Her ears were changing shape. And somehow they had moved to the top of her head.

What is happening to me? Wendy thought. She

shut her eyes, too terrified to watch the terrible changes taking place.

She felt her face twist as her nose and mouth moved closer together. The inside of her mouth became dry and strange. She touched her teeth with her tongue. Her teeth were now sharp and pointed.

"No!" she cried aloud. But this time the word came out as *Noooooowwwww!*

Wendy's heart pounded so hard she could hear it. She tried to sit up. Her balance was all wrong, and she fell off the bed. But instead of landing on her back, she landed on her feet—all *four* feet!

Terrified, Wendy jumped up on her dresser and gazed into the mirror.

She couldn't believe it. This must be a dream.

A cat gazed back at her.

A tawny-colored cat with a white star on its forehead.

Wendy turned her head. The cat in the mirror turned, too. When she lifted her hand, it lifted its front paw.

It can't be! Wendy thought. *It can't!*

But she knew the truth.

The cat in the mirror was Wendy.

Wendy was a cat.

About R. L. Stine

R. L. Stine, the creator of *Ghosts of Fear Street,* has written almost 100 scary novels for kids. The *Ghosts of Fear Street* series, like the *Fear Street* series, takes place in Shadyside and centers on the scary events that happen to people on Fear Street.

When he isn't writing, R. L. Stine likes to play pinball on his very own pinball machine, and explore New York City with his wife, Jane, and fifteen-year-old son, Matt.

Is The Roller Coaster Really Haunted?

THE BEAST

❏ 88055-1/$3.99

It Was An Awsome Ride—Through Time!

THE BEAST 2

❏ 52951-X/$3.99

 A MINSTREL® BOOK

Published by Pocket Books